If Dinosaurs Were
— Alive Today —

by Lisa Hilton & Sandra L. Kirkpatrick
Illustrated by Randy Chewning

PRICE STERN SLOAN
Los Angeles

To Christian, Grant and Alexandra

Copyright © 1988 by Lisa Hilton
Published by Price Stern Sloan, Inc.
360 North La Cienega Boulevard, Los Angeles, California 90048

ISBN: 0-8431-2309-5

10 9 8 7 6 5 4 3 2

Dinosaurs were amazing animals and they lived millions of years ago. None exist today, and no people ever saw a dinosaur. But what *if* dinosaurs were alive today?

If dinosaurs were alive today…

they would put away
a pile of burgers!

. . . .

Megalosaurus (MEG-uh-luh-SAWR-us)
was a giant meat eater with a
BIG appetite.

If dinosaurs were alive today...

they would be great marathon runners.

Deinonychus (die-noh-NY-kus)
was small and quick and raced with
the best.

If dinosaurs were alive today...

they would need help blowing out all
their birthday candles.

Iguanodon (ih-GWAN-uh-don)
was born nearly 200 million years ago
—that's a lot of candles!

If dinosaurs were alive today...

gathering Easter eggs would be a big job.

....

Triceratops (try-SER-uh-tops),
like all reptiles, hatched from eggs
—BIG eggs.

If dinosaurs were alive today...

visiting the dentist would take a very long time.

Trachodon (TRACK-uh-don)
means "rough tooth"—this dinosaur had 2,000 teeth
in rows, all close together.

If dinosaurs were alive today...

they would fall in love too.

Dimetrodons (di-MEET-row-dons),
with their large fins, may look
strange to people, but they looked
beautiful to each other.

If dinosaurs were alive today...

they would be real beach bums.

Eryops (AIR-ee-ops)
was an amphibian and needed both land
and water to be happy.

If dinosaurs were alive today...

they would go to school too.

Stegosaurus (STEG-uh-sawr-us)
was big and cute, but had
a very small brain.

If dinosaurs were alive today...

they would not need costumes to trick-or-treat.

Tyrannosaurus Rex (tie-RAN-uh-SAWR-us rex)
looked scary enough without a mask!

If dinosaurs were alive today...

they would make a special kind of music.

Lambeosaurus (lam-bee-o-SAWR-us)
honked like a horn through the crown on its head.

If dinosaurs were alive today...

they would eat everything but the Thanksgiving turkey.

Polacanthus (pol-a-KAN-thus)
was a vegetarian and didn't
eat any meat.

If dinosaurs were alive today...

they would play in the Superbowl without a uniform.

....

Protoceratops (pro-to-SER-a-tops)
was the size of a pony and
had his own face mask and
protective gear.

If dinosaurs were alive today…

they would decorate the tops of even the tallest Christmas trees.

Diplodocus (dip-PLOD-uh-kus)
stretched 30 feet above the ground and
was over 80 feet long.

If dinosaurs were alive today...

they would need a cozy spot to sleep.

. . . .

Psittacosaurus (SIT-uh-ko-sawr-us)
had to snuggle to keep warm
in cold weather—reptiles can't keep
themselves warm otherwise.